W9-BNO-234

HENDERSON DISTRICT PUBLIC LIBRARIES

3 1431 00369403 1

HENDERSON DIST PUB LIB
PASEO VERDE LIBRARY
280 S. GREEN VALLEY PKWY
HENDERSON, NV 89012
11/06/2004

BAKER & TAYLOR

Scamper
and the
Horse Show

BY
JESSIE HAAS

PICTURES BY
MARGOT APPLE

Greenwillow Books, *An Imprint of* HarperCollins*Publishers*

For Patty and Karen and Marcia Ammann
—J. H.

In loving memory of Amy Spencer and Surprise
—M. A.

Scamper and the Horse Show. Text copyright © 2004 by Jessie Haas. Illustrations copyright © 2004 by Margot Apple. All rights reserved. Manufactured in China by South China Printing Company Ltd. www.harperchildrens.com

Colored pencils were used to prepare the full-color art. The text type is Triplex Light.

Library of Congress Cataloging-in-Publication Data. Haas, Jessie. Scamper and the horse show / Jessie Haas ; pictures by Margot Apple.   p.   cm. "Greenwillow Books." Summary: Molly and her sister hope that their horse Scamper's costume will win a blue ribbon in the horse show, but some unexpected rainfall changes the situation. Includes information on horse shows. ISBN 0-06-001338-9 (trade). ISBN 0-06-001339-7 (lib. bdg.).
[1. Horse shows—Fiction. 2. Horses—Fiction. 3. Costume—Fiction. 4. Sisters—Fiction. 5. Rain and rainfall—Fiction.] I. Apple, Margot, ill. II. Title   PZ7.H11133Sc 2004 [E]—dc21 2003049068

First Edition 10 9 8 7 6 5 4 3 2 1

 Greenwillow Books

Tomorrow is the horse show.

Today we're washing Scamper.

First we have to catch him.

"Mom!"

Mom catches Scamper. We wash and wash and wash.
We rinse and rinse and rinse. We dry and dry and dry.
"Let the sun dry him more," Mom says. "If he's wet
when you let him loose, he'll roll."
"Scamper looks beautiful," Molly says. "He'll win lots
of ribbons. I want a pink ribbon."

"Blue is best," I tell her. "But Scamper can only win
 if we're good riders."
"We ride good," says Molly. "And our costume is the *best!*"
 Molly's right. Other people might ride better,
 but nobody will have a better costume.
 Scamper *is* his costume—at least partly.

Scamper feels dry to us. We let him loose.

But Scamper doesn't feel dry to himself.

He feels damp and itchy.

Scamper rolls and rolls and rolls.

Now parts of him are brown. Parts of him are green.

I don't cry, but Molly does.

"If Scamper isn't all white, our costume won't work!"

"You'll just have to wash him again," Mom says.

But not even Mom can catch Scamper now.

"There are only a few stains," Mom says.

"We'll scrub them off in the morning."

We get up early. We scrub and scrub and scrub.

"You can hardly see the green," Mom says.

"Come on, it's time to go."

The horse show is down the road, in a field.

I ride Scamper. Mom and Molly follow in the car.

My friend Patty is there with Pinky.

Pinky is thin and pink and gentle.

My friend Karen is there with Meg.

Meg is fat and golden and makes mean faces.

We lead our horses in Halter Class, then line them up.

The judge looks at them and makes marks on her card.

She hands the card to the announcer and comes back
with a set of ribbons.

Will Scamper get one? The judge gives them out—

green for sixth place, pink for fifth. Will Pinky get one?

White for fourth place, yellow for third. Will Meg?

Red for second place, blue for first.

In Halter Class, horses are supposed to be not too thin

and not too fat and perfectly clean. We don't get ribbons.

"Wait till Costume Class!" Molly says.

She rides in Lead Line Class. That's for kids too little to ride by themselves. All the little kids get purple ribbons.

Pleasure Class is for gentle horses. Scamper bucks when I tell him to canter. Pinky gets a yellow ribbon.

Equitation Class is for good riders. Scamper trots so fast I lose my stirrups. Karen gets a pink ribbon.

Now it's Trail Class. That's for brave horses
who aren't afraid of mailboxes or crossing
pretend bridges or stepping over sticks.
It's for riders who can get their horses to do
scary things. Scamper isn't afraid of anything.
We get a red ribbon.
"Hurray!" says Molly. "And in Costume we'll get a blue."

It's lunchtime. I take off Scamper's saddle. "Oh no!"
The new saddle blanket is turning Scamper's back yellow.
"Quick! Get a wet brush!" Mom says.
I dip Scamper's brush in his water bucket. I brush
and brush and brush. Scamper's back stays yellow.
"It's paler," Mom says. "The costume's so bright,
nobody will notice. Come eat lunch."
Scamper has hay and water for lunch. We have sandwiches
and cookies and juice. A big cloud comes to shade us.
A cool wind starts to blow.

Now we put on Scamper's costume. Red paper stripes
go along his sides. A blue paper blanket goes over
his rump. The blue paper has stars cut out of it.
"Look!" Patty says. "Scamper's the American flag!"
I put on a wig and hat. I'm George Washington.
Molly puts on a long dress and a thimble.
She's Betsy Ross, who sewed the first flag.
Mom takes a picture. She has to use a flash,
it's gotten so dark.

"Costume Class!" the announcer calls.
We start across the field. A red stripe rips.
Another flaps loose. Mom chases us with tape.
We're the last ones. We go through the gate,
and rain hits my face. Rain patters on my hat.
Rain flattens Scamper's blue paper blanket
and soaks the red paper stripes.

Other horses dash into horse trailers. We don't
have a horse trailer. We tie Scamper to a tree.
We sit in the car and watch.

"Our costume was the best," Molly says.

Mom hugs us both.

The rain sounds softer. "I see sunshine," Mom says.

"Look for a rainbow, girls."

"I don't see one," Molly says.

I don't either.

"Costume Class back in the ring," calls the announcer.

"Go on, girls," Mom says.

We don't want to. But Mom says, "It's part of horse shows.
You smile for the good things, and you smile for the bad."

She puts my hat on. She finds Molly's thimble. She kisses me.
She kisses Molly. She kisses Scamper. "Now, off you go!"

We line up in the ring. All the other costumes
look good. I smile at Molly. She smiles at me.
The judge walks up and down, looking.
She writes on her card and gives it to the
announcer. She comes back with the ribbons.

Green goes to the angel and pink
to the knight. The circus rider gets the white.
The headless horseman gets the yellow. Red goes to the cow.
Now just the blue ribbon is left, and the judge is walking
up to us.

"Your flag was clever," she says. "I saw it before
  the rain came. What's your costume now?"
  I look at Molly. Molly looks at me.
"A rainbow!" I say.
"A finger painting!" says Molly.
"A box of crayons?"
"A birthday cake that's been left out in the sun?"

"No, I know!" says the judge.

"A set of horse show ribbons!"

All the colors are there on Scamper—purple,

green, pink, and white, yellow and red and—

"All you need is a little bit more blue," the judge says.

She puts the blue ribbon on Scamper's bridle. "Perfect!"

More about Horse Shows

Horse shows can be huge and formal and very competitive. Or they can be small, casual, neighborhood events, held in a field or at the stable where you take riding lessons.

At some shows, horses pull carts. At others, they are ridden over jumps. There are shows for different breeds of riding horses, shows for draft horses, and shows for ponies. At some shows, people ride only English style. At some, they ride only Western.

Neighborhood horse shows are for whatever kind of riding horse or pony you happen to have. Neighborhood horse shows are often put on by 4-H Clubs or Pony Clubs. Young riders compete, and parents and grandparents cheer.

A judge decides who wins each class. Judges have to know a lot about horses and riding. They have to make up their minds quickly while many horses are circling around them.

Riders wear numbers on their arms or the backs of their jackets. As the judge chooses the winners, she writes their numbers on a card. She gives the card to the announcer.

The announcer looks at the class entry list to see what number goes with what name. Then he announces the winners over the loudspeaker. Sometimes he starts with first place and works down to sixth. Sometimes he starts with sixth and works up to first.

In Halter Class, horses are led, not ridden. They walk and trot in front of the judge. Then they stand still while she looks at them. In Halter Class, a horse should be clean and glossy and in good shape. The halter should be polished. The person leading the horse should be neatly dressed, but hard hats aren't required.

In Pleasure Class, the manner and gaits of the horses are judged. A good pleasure horse has comfortable gaits and responds quickly to the rider.

In Equitation Class, the rider's ability is what matters. The winner will be the person who sits most correctly in the saddle, handles the horse well, and makes riding look easy.

In Trail Class, horses and riders are judged on how calmly they face things they might meet on a local trail ride, like bridges, small jumps, mailboxes, and orange road cones.

Other classes are just for fun. In Lead Line, children too young to ride alone are led around on horses belonging to big brothers or sisters. For Costume Class, horse owners create costumes for themselves and their horses.

More classes that you might find at a neighborhood show include Parents Up, where grown-ups get to sit on horses and be led around by their children.

In Jumping, horses are ridden, one at a time, over a series of jumps. Barrel Racing and Pole

Bending are timed classes. Each horse races around a tight pattern of barrels or poles and is timed by someone with a stopwatch.

In the Sack Race, kids hopping inside sacks lead their horses. In Sit-a-Buck, they ride bareback,

holding a dollar bill between one leg and the horse's side. The one who keeps the dollar in place longest wins. In Egg and Spoon, riders carry eggs in kitchen spoons while they ride around the ring. (Hard-boiled eggs are used so the ring doesn't get slippery!) In the Slow Walking Race, the horse that crosses the finish line last wins.

Horse shows are exciting and sometimes upsetting for horses and riders. Riders want to show how good they are, and they want to win. Horses like to show off, too. Some like to show

the other horses how fast or how bossy they are or how hard they can buck.

Horses often behave much worse at a show than at home. Only very experienced horses do their best in a showring.

Not winning a ribbon doesn't mean you're not a good rider or your horse is not a good horse. A ribbon is just a record of how you and your horse were doing for those few moments in the class when the judge happened to be looking at you.

Horse shows are tiring for your horse. He needs a grooming, a nice roll in the dirt, and a good supper after a horse show.

When you've finished taking care of your horse, it's finally time to hang up all your ribbons.